Hairy Maclary
from Donaldson's Dairy
Lynley Dodd

GARETH STEVENS

Out of the gate
and off for a walk
went Hairy Maclary
from Donaldson's Dairy

and Hercules Morse
as big as a horse

with Hairy Maclary
from Donaldson's Dairy.

Bottomley Potts
covered in spots,
Hercules Morse
as big as a horse

and Hairy Maclary
from Donaldson's Dairy.

Muffin McLay
like a bundle of hay,
Bottomley Potts
covered in spots,
Hercules Morse
as big as a horse

and Hairy Maclary
from Donaldson's Dairy.

Bitzer Maloney
all skinny and bony,
Muffin McLay
like a bundle of hay,
Bottomley Potts
covered in spots,
Hercules Morse
as big as a horse

and Hairy Maclary
from Donaldson's Dairy.

Schnitzel von Krumm
with a very low tum,
Bitzer Maloney
all skinny and bony,
Muffin McLay
like a bundle of hay,
Bottomley Potts
covered in spots,
Hercules Morse
as big as a horse

and Hairy Maclary
from Donaldson's Dairy.

With tails in the air
they trotted on down
past the shops and the park
to the far end of town.
They sniffed at the smells
and they snooped at each door,
when suddenly,
out of the shadows
they
saw . . .

SCARFACE CLAW
the toughest Tom
in
town.

"EEEEEOWWWFFTZ!"
said Scarface Claw.

Off with a yowl
a wail and a howl,
a scatter of paws
and a clatter of claws,
went Schnitzel von Krumm
with a very low tum,
Bitzer Maloney
all skinny and bony,
Muffin McLay
like a bundle of hay,
Bottomley Potts
covered in spots,
Hercules Morse
as big as a horse

and Hairy Maclary
from Donaldson's Dairy,

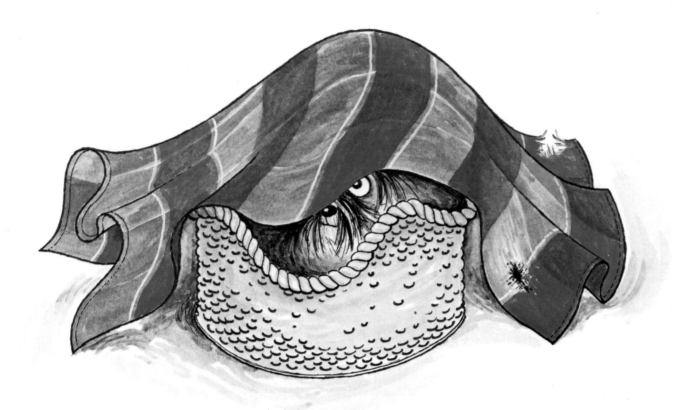

straight back home
to bed.

Acknowledgement

The publisher gratefully acknowledges the key role played by
Loren Aho Stevens, his daughter, in bringing this story to his
attention, and encouraging its publication in North America.

By Lynley Dodd:

The Nickle Nackle Tree
My Cat Likes to Hide in Boxes (with Eve Sutton)

GOLD STAR FIRST READERS

Hairy Maclary from Donaldson's Dairy   The Apple Tree
Hairy Maclary's Bone   The Smallest Turtle
Hairy Maclary Scattercat   Wake Up, Bear

Library of Congress Cataloging in Publication Data

Dodd, Lynley.
  Hairy Maclary from Donaldson's Dairy.

  Summary: A small black dog and his canine friends are
terrorized by the local tomcat.
  [1. Dogs — Fiction. 2. Cats — Fiction. 3. Bullies —
Fiction. 4. Stories in rhyme] I. Title.
PZ8.3.D637Hai 1985   [E]   85-9773
ISBN 0-918831-25-3
ISBN 0-918831-05-9 (lib. bdg.)

North American edition first published in 1985 by
Gareth Stevens, Inc.
7221 West Green Tree Road
Milwaukee, Wisconsin 53223, USA

First published by
Mallinson Rendel Publishers Ltd.

Typography by Sharon Burris.